Dear Clarence,

In searching for a way to express my gratitude to you for being my great friend I came across this book. I also think it is fitting for a special birthday of a fine person like you. It says it all.

Love always,
Kelly

D1573043

Me, the Tree

by Ann Louise Ramsey

P CROWN PEAK
PUBLICATIONS
New Castle, Colorado

P CROWN PEAK
UBLICATIONS

P.O. Box 317
New Castle, CO 81647

www.methetree.com

Library of Congress Control Number: 2004093937

ISBN 0-9645663-4-6

First Printing

Published in the United States of America

Printed in Hong Kong

**This book is dedicated to
YOU!**

*"Be true to your Soul...
no one else will, you know;
Nothing else will do,
but the life given you."*

Ann Louise Ramsey, ©2006

I also dedicate this book
to the mountain land in Western Colorado,
where I once lived,
that inspired the story in the first place.

There was a time when I was not this tall...
In fact, I was almost nothing at all...

A pine cone fell from my mother tree
And deposited the seed containing me.

Day after day, as I lay upon the ground,
The fresh winds of Autumn tossed me around...

Somehow I knew, perhaps the wind did too,
That I was just looking for the perfect view.

Where I was to live from
this moment on,
I wanted to mingle with
the moon till dawn,

Then catch the morning's
first golden thread
Of light, as Dawn's sunbeams
danced on my head,

But this meadow was
far too crowded with trees,
So I hitched a ride
on an evening breeze,

And sailed around
in my spaceship, the seed,
In search of a home
that would meet my needs.

A place that would never inhibit me,
And I could reach my potential as a tree...

Where my branches could bend,
my sap could run,
And I'd grow the finest roots
under the sun.

Look! Over there...that small meadow is bare,
Standing out in the sun and open air!

I knew it was the home I'd been searching for...
Just me in this meadow...where no tree lived before.

Plant me here, oh great and powerful Wind,
And cover me with the earth...I have reached the end...

So there I was, buried safe in the ground...
In my silent seed, I could not hear a sound;

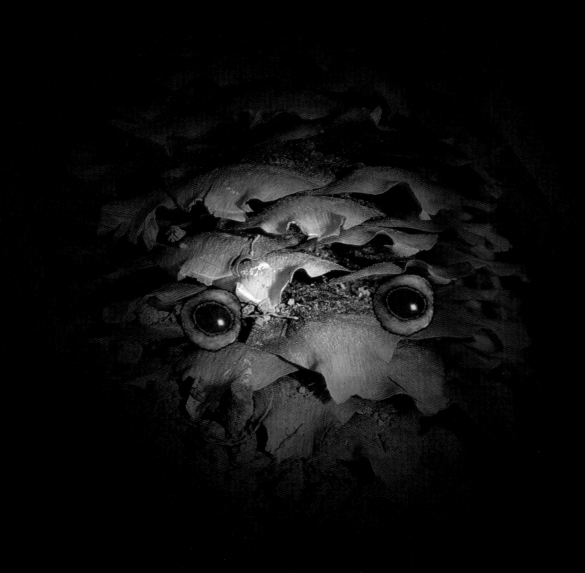

Days passed, maybe weeks...I don't really know,
But my seed would not open up to let me grow.

"Have patience," I sighed, "your time will come;
Sometimes it is later than it is for some"...

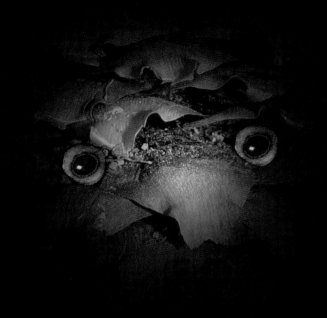

I talked myself to sleep most every night,
And spent each day in my seed looking for light.

Finally, I feared, "Maybe I'm not meant to be"...
Just then I felt the thunder shaking me;

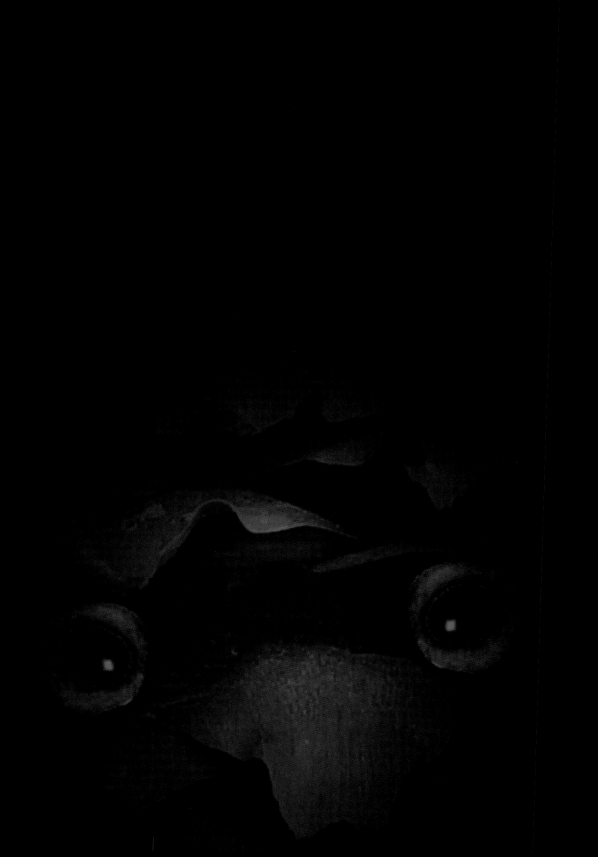

And the rain, with its life-giving power,
Soaked me in my seed with an afternoon shower.

I began to expand and break through my hard shell...
Up through the soil, I felt myself propel;

When I neared the top, I let out a shout,
And shot through the ground as a little tree sprout.

What a lot of work,
but now here I sit
On top of the ground...
definitely worth it!

I didn't know that I would be so small...
I could hardly wait for Time to make me tall.

Oh, how I worked at becoming Me!...
For I wanted so much to be a tall tree...

Before those that wandered within my short sight,
I stood as tall as I could...especially at night.

Season after season, I felt every inch
Of my branches grow, and thought, "This is a cinch"...

Patient believing,
that's the vital key
That will make me
a strong and
healthy tree.

Soon I forgot whether I was tall or small,
And felt myself being Me...that is all;

As my heart grew big with love for the sun,
I tripled my size and surprised everyone.

I felt beautiful...
a sight to behold,
As the last rays
of the sun
turned my limbs gold,

Birds sing for hours...
each melody dances
Across the meadow and
throughout my branches.

The earth has worked her magic on me...
In return for my love of being a tree,

I have gifts of flowers, birds and the rainfall...
And my love for them all has made me tall.

As the seasons change and the days come and go,
I stretch my branches over this meadow...

And the night sky, with its immense traveling show
Of glittering gems, wrapped me in indigo.

Wildflowers now bloom
all around my feet...
That scent my air
with a fragrance so sweet.

With the same wonder as the little tree sprout
That shot through the ground shouting, "Let me out!"

And after standing here for all these years,
The rain is still sweet music to my ears;

It seems the stars
shine brighter every night,
And snowflakes still fill
my branches with delight.

I give thanks to the breeze that set me free
Each time the great wind caresses me...

Not to mention, the meadow that made room
For me to grow tall and my life to bloom.

The list
is endless...
my gratitude
strong
For all the help
that I got
along...

...the way,
as I grew in the
open terrain...
From each sunbeam
to every drop
of rain.

I've grown beyond the time
when Time was all
I thought I would need
to make me tall...

Thanking each new day whose lessons teach
That my potential lies within Love's reach.

Deep in the tree that resembles me,
I touch the roots of my infinity.

Where Love's spinning circles grow and tie
All life together under one sky.